KU-275-547

A Note to Parents

DK READERS is a compelling programme for beginning readers, designed in conjunction with leading literacy experts, including Maureen Fernandes, B.Ed (Hons). Maureen has spent many years teaching literacy, both in the classroom and as a specialist in schools.

Beautiful illustrations and superb full-colour photographs combine with engaging, easy-to-read stories to offer a fresh approach to each subject in the series. Each DK READER is guaranteed to capture a child's interest while developing his or her reading skills, general knowledge and love of reading.

The five levels of DK READERS are aimed at different reading abilities, enabling you to choose the books that are exactly right for your child:

Pre-level 1: Learning to read
Level 1: Beginning to read
Level 2: Beginning to read alone
Level 3: Reading alone
Level 4: Proficient readers

The "normal" age at which a child begins to read can be anywhere from three to eight years old. Adult participation through the lower levels is very helpful for providing encouragement, discussing storylines and sounding out unfamiliar words.

No matter which level you select, you can be sure that you are helping your child learn to read, then read to learn!

Penguin Random House

For Dorling Kindersley
Editor Shari Last
Senior Slipcase Designer Mark Penfound
Senior DTP Designer Kavita Varma
Producer David Appleyard
Managing Editor Sadie Smith
Managing Art Editor Ron Stobbart
Creative Manager Sarah Harland
Art Director Lisa Lanzarini
Publisher Julie Ferris
Publishing Director Simon Beecroft

Reading Consultant Maureen Fernandes

DK India
Editor Rahul Ganguly
Senior Editor Garima Sharma
Assistant Art Editor Suzena Sengupta
Deputy Managing Art Editor Neha Ahuja
Pre-Production Manager Sunil Sharma

For Lucasfilm
Executive Editor J. W. Rinzler
Art Director Troy Alders
Keeper of the Holocron Leland Chee
Director of Publishing Carol Roeder

This edition published in 2015
First published in Great Britain in 2014 by
Dorling Kindersley Limited,
80 Strand, London, WC2R 0RL

This edition produced for The Book People,
Hall Wood Avenue, Haydock, St. Helens WA11 9UL

Slipcase UI: 001–291320–Oct/15

Page design copyright © 2015 Dorling Kindersley Limited.
A Penguin Random House Company

© and TM 2015 LUCASFILM LTD.

All rights reserved.
No part of this publication may be reproduced, stored in or introduced into a retrieval system, or transmitted, in any form, or by any means (electronic, mechanical, photocopying, recording, or otherwise), without the prior written permission of the copyright owner.

A CIP catalogue record for this book is available from the British Library

ISBN: 978-1-4093-5251-8

Printed in China.

www.starwars.com
www.dk.com

A WORLD OF IDEAS:
SEE ALL THERE IS TO KNOW

Contents

4 Hello!
6 Master Ani
8 A Quiet Life
10 Droid Mix-up
12 Cheeky Best Friend
14 Oh No… Jawas!
16 A Friendly Droid
18 The Death Star
20 Blown to Bits
22 Working for Jabba
24 Ewok Admirers
26 To the Rescue!
28 Now It's Your Turn
30 Quiz

DK READERS

BEGINNING 2 TO READ ALONE

STAR WARS™

THE ADVENTURES OF C-3PO

Written by Shari Last

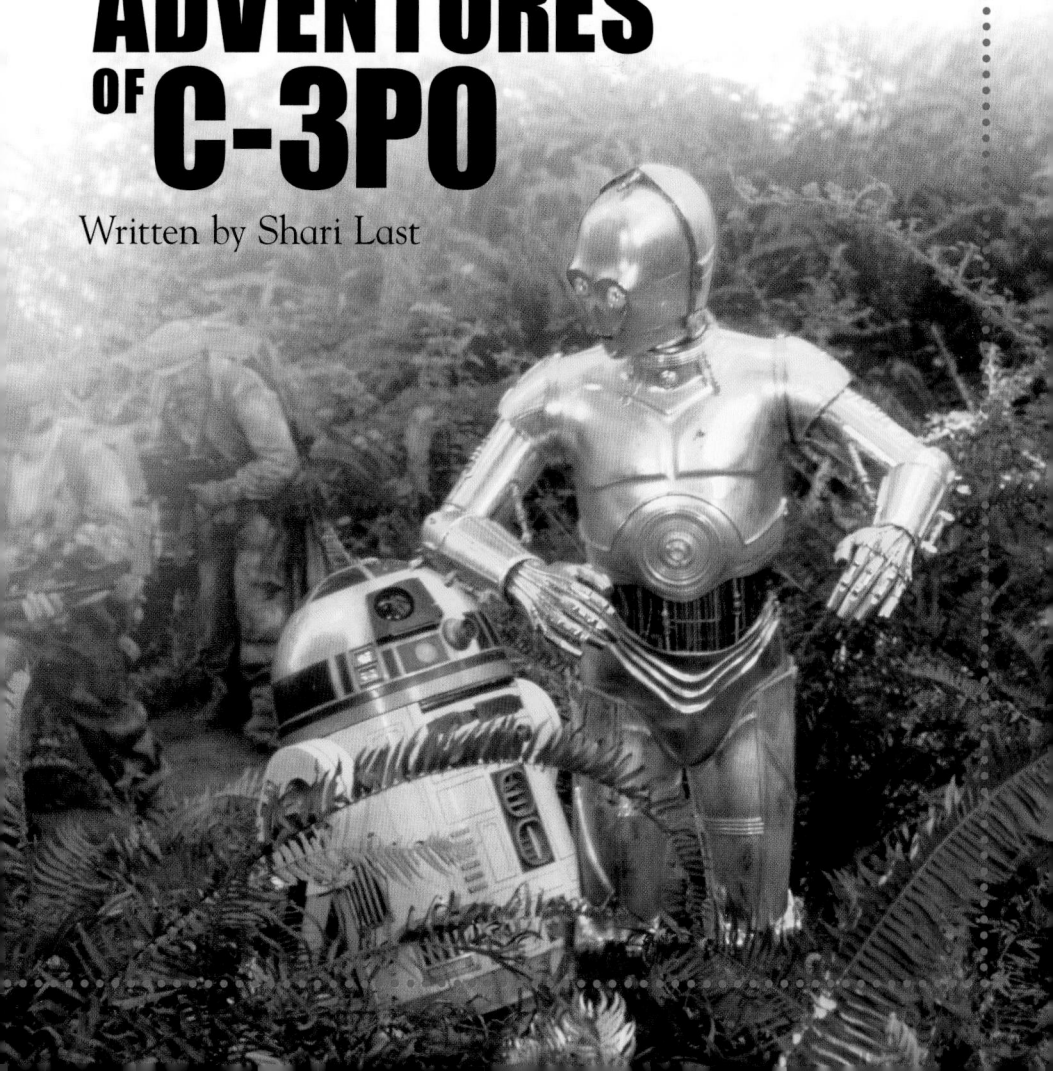

Hello!

I am C-3PO.
How may I help you?
What's that?
You don't want my help?

You want to hear
about my adventures?
Well, that is a strange request.

But, of course, I am
programmed to be of service.
Now, where shall I begin?

Master Ani

I was built on the planet Tatooine by a young slave boy named Anakin Skywalker.

I called him "Master Ani".

He wanted to build a droid helper for his mother.

Droid

A droid is a robot that is programmed to help people with certain tasks. Some droids are very clever – like C-3PO – while some are much more basic.

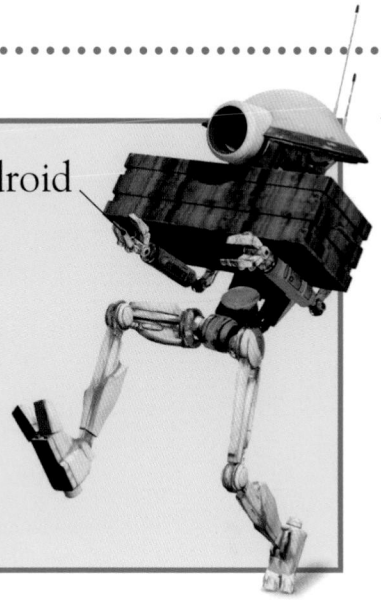

Of course, I am much cleverer than a regular droid. I can speak more than six million languages.

But I still helped Master Ani and his mother because I was a service droid and I always obeyed my master.

A Quiet Life

I like it when things are peaceful and quiet.

It gives me time to recharge my computer brain.

I am programmed to help
people communicate.
I am not built for battle.

But everything changed when
Master Ani grew older and
became a Jedi Knight. I travelled
with him to faraway planets and
joined him on many adventures!

Droid Mix-up

Once, Master Anakin and I went to the planet Geonosis where we discovered a secret droid factory.

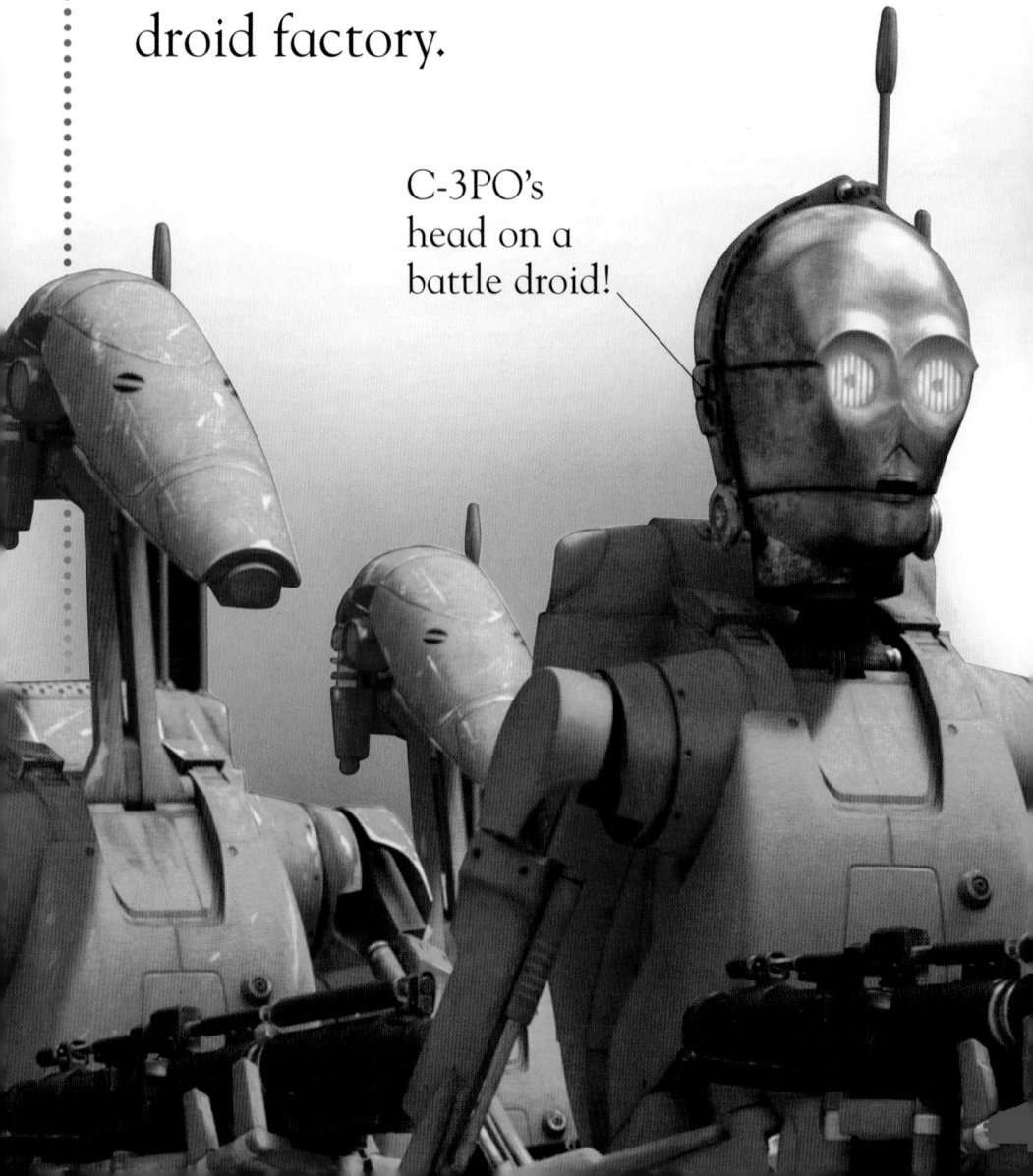

Droid factory
There are many droid factories on Geonosis. In them, huge machines build thousands of battle droids.

Unfortunately, I fell into the factory and became all mixed up with a dangerous battle droid.

I was so distressed when I found myself right in the middle of a scary battle.

Cheeky Best Friend

R2-D2 is a cheeky little
astromech droid.
We met on Tatooine and have
been best friends ever since.

R2-D2 is very brave and clever,
but he often likes to
be rude and silly!

Astromech droids
Astromech droids, such as R2-D2, are small and clever droids. They fix broken starships and help with navigation.

Don't worry. I always tell him what to do.

And he listens to me… sometimes.

Oh No... Jawas!

One of the things I hate most is getting lost. I like to feel safe.

So you can imagine how upset I was when R2-D2 and I were captured by a group of horrible Jawas.

Jawas live in the deserts of Tatooine and sell scrap metal.

First of all, I am not scrap metal. Secondly, their massive sandcrawler vehicle was very dirty!

Jawas

Jawas are small, scary creatures with glowing yellow eyes. They will sell anything they find, so don't get too close!

A Friendly Droid

I have made lots of new friends on my adventures.

Jedi Knight Luke Skywalker bought me from the Jawas. He is my new master now, but he is also my friend.

Luke's sister is Princess Leia.
She goes on secret missions to
make the galaxy a safer place.

Han Solo is a pilot.
His best friend, Chewbacca,
is a tall, hairy Wookiee.

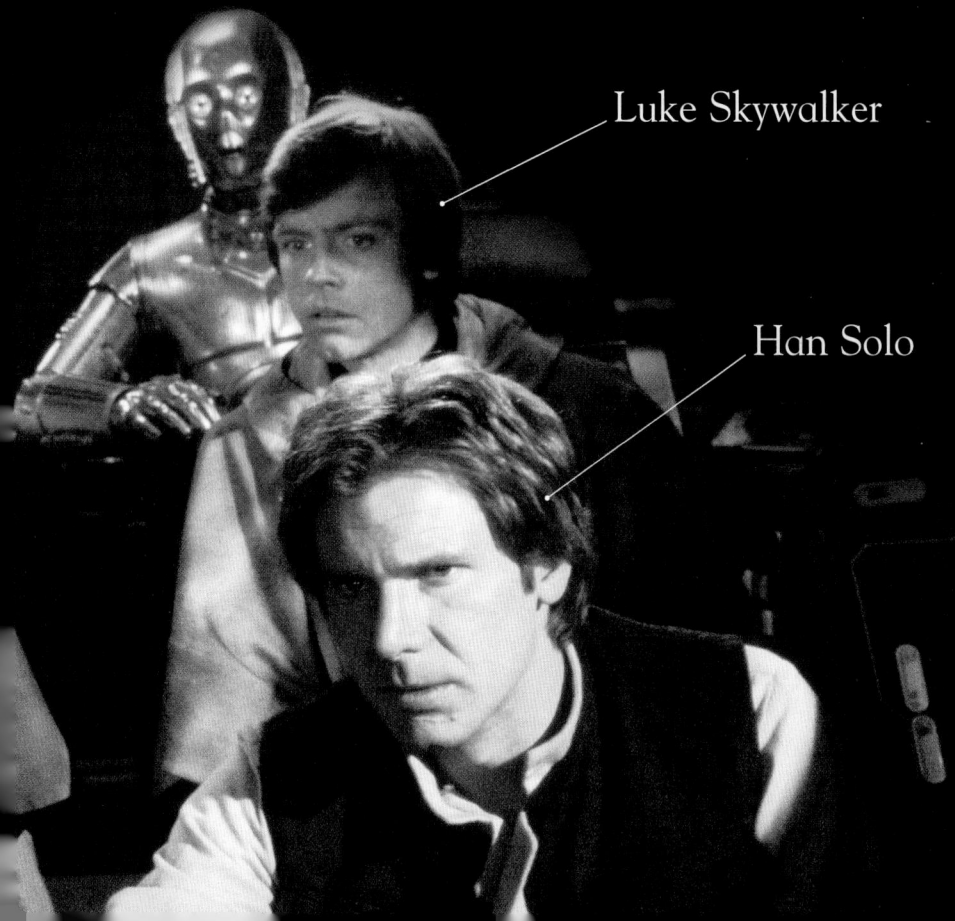

The Death Star

The Death Star is a very scary starship.

But Master Luke is not afraid of anything. We went to the Death Star to rescue a prisoner, Princess Leia.

But my friends Leia, Han and Luke got trapped in a rubbish masher, which was about to squash them!

I am proud to tell you
that I saved them.
I told R2-D2 to turn off the
rubbish masher just in time.
What a close call!

Blown to Bits

One of my worst adventures
was on Cloud City.
I walked into the wrong room –
and was blown to bits!
It was very upsetting.

Luckily, my friend Chewbacca
picked up all my pieces.
He carried me around
in a rucksack until he
had time to mend me.
Even though he made a few
mistakes when putting me back
together, I was very grateful.

Working for Jabba

Jabba the Hutt is a big, slimy, disgusting creature!
He loves capturing and bothering innocent people.

He captured me once and forced me to be his translator. I hated it!

When I worked for Jabba, I was treated with no respect – even by his pet, Salacious Crumb!

I was very pleased when Master Luke defeated Jabba and rescued me.

Salacious Crumb
This is Jabba's favourite pet. He must make Jabba laugh at least once a day or he will be in big trouble.

Ewok Admirers

I often think that none of my friends truly appreciate how wonderful and special I am. The Ewoks do, though.

Ewoks are small, tough creatures who live on the forest moon of Endor.

The Ewoks were fascinated by my shiny gold body. They listened to everything I said, and they helped my friends and me on our mission.

To the Rescue!

Once, R2-D2 and I were hiding in the forest of Endor when a group of stormtroopers captured our friends.

I wanted to help my friends, so I shouted to the stormtroopers and they came chasing after me.

But I tricked them! When they came near, an army of Ewoks jumped out of the trees and helped us defeat the stormtroopers. Hooray!

Stormtroopers

Stormtroopers are soldiers who work for an evil Empire. They wear white armour and carry deadly blasters.

Now It's Your Turn

My favourite part of an adventure is the end. I am happy because then it is time to sit down again and relax… before the next adventure begins.

But remember, you don't have to fly in starships or travel around the galaxy to have amazing adventures.

You can go on an exciting adventure wherever you are!

Quiz

1. On which planet are the droid factories?

2. Who is C-3PO's best friend?

3. What creatures sell scrap metal on Tatooine?

4. Where was Princess Leia held prisoner?

5.Who is Jabba the Hutt's pet?

Answers:
1. Geonosis
2. R2-D2
3. Jawas
4. On the Death Star
5. Salacious Crumb

Index

Anakin Skywalker 6, 7, 9
astromech droid 12

battle droid 10, 11

Chewbacca 16, 17, 21
Cloud City 21

Death Star 18
droid factory 10, 11

Endor 25, 26
Ewoks 25, 27

Geonosis 10, 11

Han Solo 17, 18

Jabba 22, 23
Jawas 14, 15
Jedi Knight 9, 16

Luke Skywalker 16, 17, 18, 23

Princess Leia 16, 17, 18

R2-D2 12, 14, 19, 26

Salacious Crumb 23
stormtroopers 26, 27

Tatooine 6, 12, 14

Wookiee 17